Fascinating Insects

Bumblebees

Aaron Carr

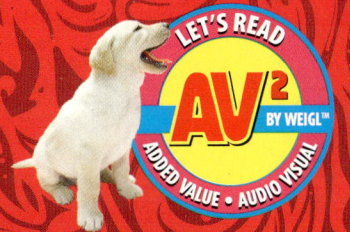

www.av2books.com

LET'S READ
AV² BY WEIGL
ADDED VALUE • AUDIO VISUAL

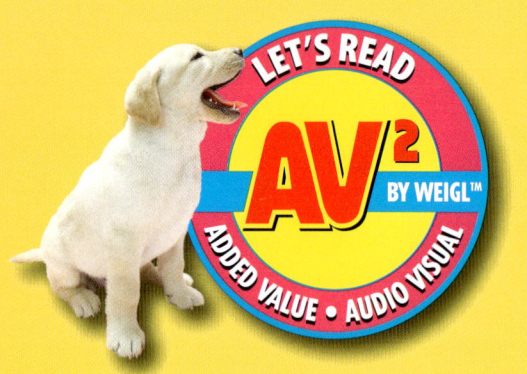

Go to www.av2books.com, and enter this book's unique code.

BOOK CODE

X850455

AV² by Weigl brings you media enhanced books that support active learning.

AV² provides enriched content that supplements and complements this book. Weigl's AV² books strive to create inspired learning and engage young minds in a total learning experience.

Your AV² Media Enhanced books come alive with...

Audio
Listen to sections of the book read aloud.

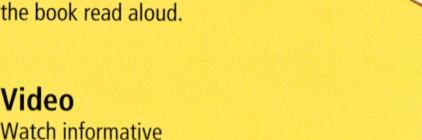

Video
Watch informative video clips.

Embedded Weblinks
Gain additional information for research.

Try This!
Complete activities and hands-on experiments.

Key Words
Study vocabulary, and complete a matching word activity.

Quizzes
Test your knowledge.

Slide Show
View images and captions, and prepare a presentation.

... and much, much more!

Published by AV² by Weigl
350 5th Avenue, 59th Floor New York, NY 10118
Websites: www.av2books.com www.weigl.com

Copyright ©2015 AV² by Weigl
All rights reserved. No part of this publication may be reproduced, stored in a retrieval system, or transmitted in any form or by any means, electronic, mechanical, photocopying, recording, or otherwise, without the prior written permission of the publisher.

Library of Congress Cataloging-in-Publication Data

Carr, Aaron.
Bumblebees / Aaron Carr.
    pages cm -- (Fascinating insects)
ISBN 978-1-4896-1034-8 (hardcover : alk. paper) -- ISBN 978-1-4896-1035-5 (softcover : alk. paper) --
ISBN 978-1-4896-1036-2 (single-user ebook) -- ISBN 978-1-4896-1037-9 (multi-user ebook)
1. Bumblebees--Juvenile literature. I. Title.
 QL568.A6C29 2014
 595.79'9--dc 3
                                    2014002367

Printed in the United States of America in North Mankato, Minnesota
1 2 3 4 5 6 7 8 9 0   18 17 16 15 14

032014
WEP150314

Project Coordinator: Aaron Carr   Art Director: Terry Paulhus

Weigl acknowledges Getty Images as the primary image supplier for this title.

Bumblebees

CONTENTS

2 AV² Book Code
4 Meet the Bumblebee
6 Where They Live
8 Living in Groups
10 Life Cycle
12 Growing Up
14 Staying Safe
16 How Bees Fly
18 What They Eat
20 Role in Nature
22 Bumblebee Facts
24 Key Words/AV2books.com

Meet the bumblebee.

Bumblebees are small insects.
They are known for their round bodies with black and yellow stripes.

Bumblebees are found in most parts of the world.

In most parts of the world, bumblebees live in warm places.

7

Bumblebees live in large groups.

These large groups are called colonies.

Bumblebees are born when they hatch from eggs.

When they hatch from eggs, bumblebees are small and white.

Baby bumblebees wrap themselves in cocoons.

12

In cocoons, baby bumblebees change into full-grown bumblebees.

Bumblebees have stingers.

Stingers help bumblebees keep themselves safe.

16

Bumblebees have four wings to help them fly.

Their four wings make a buzzing sound when they flap.

Bumblebees eat pollen and nectar from flowers.

Pollen and nectar from flowers give bumblebees everything they need to be healthy.

19

Bumblebees are important in nature.

In nature, bumblebees help make new flowers.

21

BUMBLEBEE FACTS

These pages provide more detail about the interesting facts found in the book. They are intended to be used by adults as a learning support to help young readers round out their knowledge of each insect or arachnid featured in the *Fascinating Insects* series.

Pages 4–5

Bumblebees are small insects. Insects are small animals with segmented bodies and six jointed legs. Their bodies are covered with hard outer shells, called exoskeletons, with three parts: the head, thorax, and abdomen. There are about 250 species of bumblebees. The bumblebee has a short, round body that can be up to 1 inch (2.5 centimeters) long and weigh as much as 0.03 ounces (0.85 grams) for the largest bees, called queens.

Pages 6–7

Bumblebees are found in most parts of the world. They can be found in North and South America, Europe, and Asia. Bumblebees have also been introduced to New Zealand. Most bumblebees live in temperate climates in the northern hemisphere. Aside from the polar regions, the only major parts of the world that are not home to bumblebees are Africa and parts of India.

Pages 8–9

Bumblebees live in large groups. Each group, or colony, is started by a queen each spring. The queen chooses a spot for the nest and begins laying eggs. The first bees born are workers. Workers are females who do all of the work for the colony. They protect the nest, gather pollen and nectar, and take care of the young. Male bees, or drones, and new queens are born in late summer. A new queen mates with a drone and then hibernates before winter. She will begin a new colony the following spring.

Pages 10–11

Bumblebees are born when they hatch from eggs. There are four stages to the bumblebee's life cycle: egg, larva, pupa, and adult. The queen begins by laying each egg into its own cell, which is made of wax. After hatching from the egg, the bumblebee larva looks like a small, white worm. Older bees feed pollen and nectar to the larva in its waxy cell. The larva eats and grows for two weeks.

Pages 12–13

Baby bumblebees wrap themselves in cocoons. Inside the wax cell, the bumblebee larva spins a cocoon of silk around itself. The growing bumblebee is now a pupa. Inside the cocoon, the pupa begins to go through a process of change called metamorphosis. The fully-grown adult bumblebee comes out of the cocoon and leaves its wax cell. The whole process, from hatching egg to adult bee, takes about four to five weeks.

Pages 14–15

Bumblebees have stingers. Only female bumblebees have stingers, including both the workers and the queen. Unlike other types of bees, such as honeybees, bumblebees do not have barbs on their stingers. This means they can sting more than once. The stinger is used to protect the bumblebees and their nest from potential threats, such as other insects, animals, or people. Bumblebee predators include wasps, birds, and spiders.

Pages 16–17

Bumblebees have four wings. They have two large front wings and two smaller rear wings. The front and rear wings on each side of the body are connected through tiny hooks called hamuli. Bumblebees are one of the most inefficient fliers of all insects. This is because their small wings have to work harder to keep their large bodies in the air. The bumblebee's rapid wing flapping, along with its vibrating wing muscles and thorax, makes a distinct buzzing sound when it flies.

Pages 18–19

Bumblebees eat pollen and nectar from flowers. Pollen gives bumblebees the proteins and nutrients they need to grow and stay healthy, while nectar provides the energy needed to fly and work. Bumblebees sometimes make small balls of pollen with a bit of nectar. This is known as bee bread. Bumblebees also make honey, but only enough to feed the colony. First, the bees collect nectar from flowers. Then, they swallow the nectar, regurgitate it, and chew it until it becomes thick and sticky.

Pages 20–21

Bumblebees are important in nature. By collecting pollen and nectar from flowers, bees help flowers to reproduce. This process is called pollination, and bumblebees are some of the best pollinators in the world. By helping flowers reproduce, bumblebees play an important role in the food chain. However, the number of wild flowers is declining in many places where bumblebees live. This makes it harder for them to find the food they need to survive.

KEY WORDS

Research has shown that as much as 65 percent of all written material published in English is made up of 300 words. These 300 words cannot be taught using pictures or learned by sounding them out. They must be recognized by sight. This book contains 39 common sight words to help young readers improve their reading fluency and comprehension. This book also teaches young readers several important content words. These words are paired with pictures to aid in learning and improve understanding.

Page	Sight Words First Appearance
4	the
5	and, are, for, small, their, they, with
6	found, in, live, most, of, parts, places, world
8	groups, large
9	these
10	from, when
11	white
13	change, into
14	have
15	help, keep
16	a, four, make, sound, them, to
18	eat
19	be, give, need
20	important, new

Page	Content Words First Appearance
4	bumblebee
5	bodies, insects, stripes
9	colonies
10	eggs
12	cocoons
14	stingers
16	wings
18	flowers, nectar, pollen
20	nature

Check out www.av2books.com for activities, videos, audio clips, and more!

1. Go to www.av2books.com.
2. Enter book code. **X 8 5 0 4 5 5**
3. Fuel your imagination online!

www.av2books.com